Vikings Don't Wear Wrestling Belts DISCARDED

by **Debbie Dadey**
and
Marcia Thornton Jones

illustrated by **John Steven Gurney**

A
LITTLE APPLE
PAPERBACK

SCHOLASTIC INC.
New York   Toronto   London   Auckland   Sydney
Mexico City   New Delhi   Hong Kong

For the wonderful kids and teachers in Chicago.
—DD

To Janice Schweitzer — Thank you for using
"brainpower" to help me "wrestle" with all those
writing woes! — MTJ

No part of this publication may be reproduced in whole or in part, or stored in a retrieval system, or transmitted in any form or by any means, electronic, mechanical, photocopying, recording, or otherwise, without written permission of the publisher. For information regarding permission, write to Scholastic Inc., Attention: Permissions Department, 555 Broadway, New York, NY 10012.

ISBN 0-439-21583-8

12 11 10 9 8 7 6 5 4 3 2 1   1 2 3 4 5 6/0

Printed in the U.S.A.   40

First Scholastic printing, January 2001

Contents

1

WrestleBaileyLive

"What's going on at the high school?" Melody asked as she walked past the school with her friends Howie, Liza, and Eddie.

"It looks like a little excitement," Eddie said. "Let's check it out."

The kids crossed Delaware Boulevard to get closer. Fifteen parents carried signs in front of Bailey City High School. The signs said in big green letters: SAY NO TO WRESTLING!

"Isn't that your mom?" Melody asked Liza.

"There's my mother, too," Howie said. "What's going on?"

Liza pointed to a poster on a lamppost. "This explains everything," Liza told her

friends. The kids huddled around to read the brightly colored sign.

WRESTLEBAILEYLIVE
This Friday and Saturday
at Bailey City High School
See the Champion Viking Vince
Take on All Challengers!

"Our parents are protesting against these wrestling matches," Howie said.

Eddie took off his baseball cap and waved it in front of Howie's nose. "Your parents don't know what's fun. I think wrestling is exciting."

"My mother says wrestling is a bad example for kids," Howie told his friends, knocking Eddie's cap away from his nose.

Liza nodded. "My mom is going to complain to the school board."

"She can't do that!" Eddie yelled. "I've never seen a live wrestling match before. I can't wait to see *WrestleBaileyLive.*"

"Your grandmother would never let you go," Liza told Eddie.

Eddie put his hands on his hips. "I can do anything I want," he bragged.

"That's not true, and you know it," Melody said.

"Besides, *WrestleBaileyLive* is not real wrestling," Liza explained to Eddie. "They just pretend to do that stuff."

"It's all make-believe," Howie agreed.

"Well, if it's make-believe, then why does anyone need to complain about it?" Eddie asked.

His three friends thought for a moment. Liza tossed her blond ponytail behind her and said, "Some people like professional wrestling and some don't. My mom definitely doesn't like it."

"But if your goody-goody parents keep this up, the high school might really cancel *WrestleBaileyLive*," Eddie worried. "It's not fair to the people who like it."

"Eddie has a point," Melody said.

"After all, professional wrestling can be fun to watch."

Liza's mouth dropped open. Howie looked like he was ready to faint. "You mean," Howie said slowly, "that *you* like wrestling?"

Melody shrugged.

Howie opened his mouth to speak when a huge shadow fell over the kids. They shivered and turned to face a mountain of a man.

2

Viking Vince

A man with muscles the size of watermelons towered over the four friends. The kids looked up, up, and up until they finally saw his head. He had on a leather hat, but long strands of wavy hair the color of straw poked out. He wore a long heavy cape fastened over his right shoulder with a giant red button. Liza noticed that the button changed colors when the man moved.

The man's huge body blocked out the sun. Howie backed up three steps. Melody gasped. Liza hid behind Melody. Eddie grinned up at the stranger. Even though the kids were in his shadow, the large, muscular man didn't seem to notice the kids at all. He was too busy glaring at the parents marching in circles in front of the school.

Eddie tugged on the man's cape and asked, "Are you a wrestler?" The man snarled down at Eddie as if he were an ant to stomp on.

"I am Vince," the man said, his voice reminding Melody of a tiger's growl. "Viking Vince the Invincible."

"You're kidding, right?" Eddie said with a laugh. "After all, Vikings didn't wear hats. They wore helmets with horns so big they would make a bull jealous."

The giant of a man glared down at Eddie and snarled. "I am never dishonest," he told Eddie with a voice as cold as ice. "Besides, true Vikings never place nonsense such as horns on their helmets."

Viking Vince turned to leave, his cape swirling like a black cloud. Something at his waist caught the light of the sun.

Howie gasped as the wrestler marched around the building and out of sight.

"Did you see that?" Howie asked his friends. "I think he was wearing a sword under his cape."

"Don't be ridiculous," Melody said. "Wrestlers don't wear swords."

"No," Howie said seriously, "but real Vikings do!"

3

Warrior

"Vikings!" Liza shrieked. "Weren't they warriors who sailed the oceans to raid unsuspecting victims?"

Howie nodded. "Exactly."

Melody said, "It makes sense. Vince's cape and snarl are part of his act. Everyone knows that wrestlers dress up in costumes and pretend to be really mean."

"It worked for me," Liza said. "He scared my toenails off."

"Let's follow him," Eddie suggested. "Maybe we can ask him about wrestling."

"Are you crazy?" Howie asked. "Vince might eat us for dinner."

Melody laughed. "We wouldn't even be a good snack for him. Especially Eddie, because he's so sour."

"Very funny, lemon-head," Eddie said

with a snarl of his own. "I plan on getting a better look at the sword Howie was talking about." Before his friends could argue, Eddie took off, hot on Vince's trail.

Liza shook her head. "I wish Eddie would think before he does crazy things."

"Come on," Howie said. "Let's find him before he gets in trouble."

The three friends followed Eddie, keeping close to the building so the picketing parents wouldn't see them. They slipped around the building to a parking lot and came to a dead stop.

"Where did all these trailers come from?" Liza asked.

Howie shrugged. "They must belong to the wrestlers."

The kids stared at the trailers. Each one was decorated differently. One had drawings of snakes all over it, while another trailer was painted to look like an animal's cage with a huge bear claw hanging over its doorway. There was a

11

trailer that looked like a cave and another covered with a jungle mural.

Melody snapped her fingers. "Each wrestler must have his own trailer," she said. "One of these belongs to The Viper and the next one must be where Bear Claw hangs out. I bet that trailer is for the CaveMonster and the one next to it belongs to Apeman of the Jungle."

Liza and Howie stared at Melody. "How do you know all that?" Liza finally asked.

Melody gave her friends a little smile.
"Every once in a while I happen to see it
on television. It really isn't all that bad.
Not when you know it's just for fun."

They found Eddie pounding on a door
to a small trailer at the end of the line.
The trailer looked like an old sailing ship
sitting on wheels. The sides of the trailer
were made of rough carved wood. A
mast complete with sail towered above
the trailer. A big star painted on the door

13

read VIKING VINCE. Underneath his name it read CURRENT CHAMPION.

Eddie was banging on Viking Vince's door when his three friends finally caught up to him. "Eddie, get away from there," Howie snapped, but Eddie didn't listen. He knocked again. This time, the door creaked open all on its own.

"Don't go inside," Liza squealed.

"I'm just going to take a quick look," Eddie said. "The door is open. It's not like I'm breaking in or anything."

Eddie took one step inside the trailer, with his friends right behind him. "I've never seen anything so weird looking," Eddie whispered.

"Don't you remember our history lesson?" Howie asked. "This is all Viking stuff."

The kids were quiet as they looked around the trailer. Rough boards covered the walls and pictures of sea creatures hung everywhere. Gold chains and silver watches filled an entire table. Four huge television sets and stereo equipment of every kind were crammed beside stacks of video games and movies.

"Cool," Eddie said. "This looks like somebody won the lottery."

"Why would one person need so many televisions?" Melody asked.

"And where did he get all this jewelry?" Liza asked as she dipped her hand through the gold and silver.

"Forget about the jewels," Howie gasped, "and look at that!"

4

Runes

On the far side of the room, a trophy case was tucked in the corner. Each shelf was filled with mysterious statues made from big chunks of rock. The statues were etched with strange symbols and designs, but they were not what had caught Howie's attention.

A huge display of ancient-looking shields and broadaxes took up one end of the room. "Awesome," Eddie said and headed toward the axes, but a deep voice from a back room stopped him dead in his tracks. "Ahoy there. Who invades my territory?"

Viking Vince made his way from a back room. His shoulders were so wide he had to turn sideways to go through the narrow doorway. He no longer wore his

cape. The kids had never met anybody wearing so much gold and silver. He wore a ring on every finger and a bunch of chains were draped over his neck. Even his leather vest was fastened with an unusual gold pin. But what really caught their eyes was the huge belt strapped around his waist.

"There's your sword," Eddie said in a disappointed whisper. "It's nothing but a stupid belt."

This was no ordinary belt. Viking Vince's gold-and-silver belt was so wide it covered half of his stomach. "That's his wrestling belt," Melody said softly. "He's the defending champion."

"We weren't bothering anything," Howie told Viking Vince.

Eddie pushed in front of Melody. "We just came to sign up as wrestlers!" Eddie flexed an arm muscle, trying to impress Viking Vince.

Vince peered down at Eddie and laughed, but it wasn't a friendly laugh at all. "You're not quite ready for the wrestling ring," Vince said, his voice carrying an accent that rolled like ocean waves.

"But I'm the strongest kid in Bailey City," Eddie bragged.

Liza couldn't help but giggle. "That would be true if you were the *only* kid in Bailey City!"

"Who might you be?" Vince asked.

Liza held out her hand. "I'm Liza, and these are my friends Melody, Eddie, and Howie. Eddie is the one who likes telling tall tales," Liza said. "It's nice to meet you."

"You obviously aren't from Bailey City," Howie said. "I've never heard an accent like yours before."

Vince ignored Liza's hand and pointed to a map on the wall by the axes. "I call the cold waters of Scandinavia my homeland," he said.

Eddie didn't care about names and places. He was interested in wrestling.

19

"Can you teach me a few moves to use on playground bullies?" he asked. "And maybe a headlock for teachers who give me too much homework?"

Vince shook his head. "Wrestling isn't for playgrounds and classrooms," he growled. "It's a sport that should stay in the ring with a referee. That's the only way to prove you're invincible. Come to the main event on Saturday and you will see me win!"

"How do you know you'll win?" Melody asked suspiciously.

"Because Invincible is my name," Vince said with a smile. "And I always live up to my name."

"Nobody can win all the time," Liza pointed out.

Vince put his hands on his wide belt and laughed a deep, rolling laugh. "Maybe not most landlubbers," he said. "But this belt proves I am the best. No one has been able to strip me of my title. Nobody." Vince pointed to the trophy

case full of rock statues. "My life is a tale of winning and my runes prove it."

"I have a yard full of rocks," Eddie said. "They don't prove a thing."

Vince gently lifted a statue from its shelf and held it so the kids could see the strange etchings. "These are not ordinary rocks," he said. "They tell my stories, every one an adventure."

"What happened to the statue on the top?" Howie asked, pointing to the empty shelf in the trophy case.

Vince grinned. "That is where my next victory rune will be placed," he said.

Melody leaned close to the statue in Vince's hand. "Those aren't regular letters," she said. "What do they say?"

Vince carefully placed the statue back on the shelf. "Perhaps I will share what these runes say another time," he said. "But this I will tell you now. I am Invincible Vince and I am prepared to invade Bailey City!"

5

Viking Pirates

"We've got to see all the matches this weekend," Eddie said as the kids walked around the high school gym.

"I don't think there will be any matches," Melody said, pointing to the group of parents who were still in front of the gym. Two police cars with flashing lights pulled up beside the parents.

"Wrestling is not for young kids," Liza said. "It's not safe."

"Especially," Howie said slowly, "when one of the wrestlers is a Viking planning to take over the entire city."

"Vince wasn't talking about taking over the city," Melody said. "He meant he planned to win *WrestleBaileyLive*."

"I'm not so sure," Howie said. "Real Vikings explored new worlds."

Liza nodded. "We know all about explorers. Remember when Mrs. Jeepers made us learn about Christopher Columbus and Lewis and Clark."

"Exactly," Howie said. "Now you see what I mean."

"The only thing I see is that your mind has gone exploring the deep sea," Eddie told his friend.

"Eddie has a point," Melody said as she leaned against a lamppost. "What do famous explorers have to do with a wrestler in Bailey City?"

"Explorers charted new territory for one major reason," Howie told his friends. "Money."

"That's true," Liza said, nodding thoughtfully. "Christopher Columbus and the Lewis and Clark expedition were looking for trade routes."

"Vikings were no different," Howie pointed out. "They were excellent explorers and sailors, but lots of folks hated them because they thought they were mean pirates who would stop at nothing when raiding for silver and gold."

Eddie rubbed his hands together. "Now you're talking. For a minute there you were boring me to tears. You sounded just like a teacher giving a history lesson. But pirates hunting gold and silver sounds like an adventure."

"Maybe for the Vikings it was an adventure," Melody said thoughtfully. "But I bet the people the Vikings robbed believed they were horrible and mean."

Howie held up his hand to stop Melody. "Vikings may have been vicious pirates," he told her, "but they were known for their honesty and loyalty."

"How do you know so much about Vikings?" Liza asked Howie.

"I watched a program on the History Channel about them last week," Howie explained.

"Hey, Howie's not the only smart kid around," Eddie bragged. "I know a little bit about Vikings, too."

Liza, Melody, and Howie looked at Eddie in surprise. "How did you learn about Vikings?" Melody asked.

"By reading an encyclopedia," Eddie said smugly.

Howie gasped. Melody gulped. Eddie was not known for doing anything educational unless he had to.

Finally, Howie swallowed and said, "*You* read an encyclopedia?"

Eddie shrugged. "My grandmother made me. She got mad at me for telling a lie after I ate all her peanut butter cookies. I told her that an army of ants invaded the kitchen and carried away all the cookies. She made me copy an entire page out of an encyclopedia. She figured I might as well learn something if I had to be punished. I had to copy everything about Vikings."

"Did you learn anything?" Liza asked, her eyes wide.

Eddie scratched his red hair and tried

to remember. "Well, I do remember that one Viking got lost and found America."

"I thought Christopher Columbus discovered America," Liza said.

Eddie shook his head. "History is all jumbled up. How does anybody know who was really here first?"

"I know the answer to that," Melody said. "The Native Americans were here first, so I guess they really discovered America."

"See?" Eddie said. "History is confusing. Here's something else that didn't make sense from the encyclopedia page. Vikings wrote about their adventures using weird symbols engraved on rocks."

"That sounds like the rocks in Viking Vince's trailer," Liza said slowly.

"Exactly!" Howie shrieked. His face turned as pale as the clouds in the sky. "And those symbols were called runes. Don't you know what this means?" he asked his friends.

Liza, Melody, and Eddie shook their heads.

Howie gulped before telling his friends. "Invincible Vince really is a Viking who has come to conquer Bailey City!"

6

Sting Like a Bee

"It's totally awesome," Eddie told his friends as they gathered under the oak tree on the playground after school the next day. "Wouldn't it be cool if Viking Vince were a real Viking?"

"But he's not," Liza said. "He's just a strange guy who wears underwear and a cape to work every day."

"Don't forget his big wrestling belt," Howie added.

"And Eddie thought he could wrestle Vince himself," Liza said with a giggle.

Melody laughed out loud. "If Eddie tried on Vince's wrestling belt, he'd fall right over!"

Eddie's face turned red as he leaned against the oak tree. "Stop making fun.

I'm serious. Didn't you hear Viking Vince brag about invading Bailey City?"

"You are an expert on telling tales," Melody told Eddie. "You should know Vince was only bragging about the wrestling world."

"All this wrestling talk is giving me a headache," Liza moaned.

Melody patted Liza on the arm. "I bet a delicious Doodlegum Shake will make you feel better."

Eddie jumped away from the tree and started dancing around. "Let's go," Eddie said. "I need energy if I'm going to float like a butterfly and sting like a bee."

Howie laughed. "That's from a famous boxer, not a wrestler."

"Who cares?" Eddie said. "Let's go get some shakes."

The four headed to Burger Doodle for their favorite Doodlegum Shakes. As soon as they walked in the door, Eddie marched up to the owner. "I need to bulk

up by slurping a shake," he said to Mrs. Scott. Eddie held up a puny arm as proof.

"Now why would a young man like you want to build such big muscles?" she asked.

"Because," Eddie explained, "I plan to be a wrestler."

Mrs. Scott's face turned as pale as vanilla ice cream. "Baahhhh," she said. "I hope never to hear the word *wrestling* in my store again. Don't you children know brainpower is better than brute strength any day?" With that, Mrs. Scott turned away from the kids and mixed them each a milk shake.

The kids slid into a corner booth just as the door to Burger Doodle swung open. Melody, Liza, Eddie, and Howie looked up to see Invincible Vince blocking the door, and he wasn't alone.

7

Viking Invasion

Three Vikings followed Vince into Burger Doodle. They all wore capes and leather hats like Vince, but their heads only reached his shoulders. Vince towered over them.

"Oh, no," Liza squealed. "We're being invaded."

"Hide," Howie hissed. The four kids slid down in their seats until their heads were well below the booth. They peeked over the top of their seats to see Vince and his followers toss their capes into a booth not far from theirs. All the Vikings wore layers of silver and gold chains, but Vince was the only one with a heavy wrestling belt.

"They must be Vince's manager and trainers," Melody whispered. Suddenly

34

the door burst open and more wrestlers and their managers poured into Burger Doodle. One of the wrestlers had lobster claws hanging on a necklace around his neck. "Is he crazy?" Liza squealed softly, grabbing Melody's arm.

"Not as nuts as that one." Melody motioned to a large woman who had a live snake wrapped around her waist.

Howie shook his head. He'd never seen so many costumes except at Halloween. The only person without a costume was a small woman with a camera. "She's from the Bailey City newspaper," Howie whispered to his friends.

"Give me five Double Onion Doodle Burgers," growled Vince to the owner of Burger Doodle.

"He must really be hungry," Eddie whispered.

"He's probably ordering for his friends, too," Howie explained. But Howie was wrong. Each Viking ordered five Double Onion Doodle Burgers, as well as fries and shakes. The rest of the wrestlers sat down and started eating, but not Vince and his friends. They attacked their food. The Vikings were so busy gobbling Double Onion Doodle Burgers that they didn't notice the four kids spying on them.

Liza held her stomach when Vince crammed an entire burger into his mouth. "That's disgusting," she said softly.

"Cool," Eddie said. "I wonder if I could do that."

One of Vince's Vikings threw back his

head and gulped down a whole shake. "Don't they have any manners?" Melody whispered.

"Wrestlers don't have to worry about manners," Eddie said.

"Neither do Vikings," Howie said. "Eddie's grandmother would have a heart attack if she saw them."

As if to prove Howie right, Vince burped so loudly Liza put her hands over her ears, but that didn't stop her from seeing Vince's manager knock over an

entire container of french fries. Another one of the Vikings started eating them off the floor.

"Yuck!" Liza said.

"Where did the owner go?" Howie asked, turning away from Vince. "She should do something about these Viking slobs."

"Mrs. Scott must be grilling more burgers," Melody decided.

"Or she's hiding," Eddie pointed out.

"Do you mean we're surrounded by these crazy wrestlers and there is no one here to protect us?" Liza whined.

"Never fear," Eddie said. "I'll protect you."

"You and what army?" Melody hissed.

"We'll be safe," Howie assured his friends with a finger to his lips, "as long as they don't find out we're here."

"Shh," Melody warned. "Vince is talking."

Vince stood up. When he did, a few french fries were ground into mush under his foot. Vince banged his cup on the table until the rest of the wrestlers were quiet. "I have traveled great distances and across the boundaries of time for this very moment," he told the other wrestlers. "Now victory is at hand. Bailey City will be mine!"

The three other Vikings lifted their cups high in the air and cheered.

The newspaper reporter snapped pictures of Viking Vince parading around the restaurant and showing off his wrestling belt. Vince's trainers and manager stood up to cheer Vince again, but the rest of the wrestlers booed loudly.

One wrestler did more than boo. He roared. The wrestler with a huge bearskin draped over his head and shoulders stood up. His growl made Liza spill her shake right into Howie's lap.

"I've seen him on TV before," Melody whispered. "His name is Bear Claw."

"No kidding," Eddie said. "I thought his name was Tinkerbell."

Bear Claw roared again and pounded on his chest. He marched up to Viking Vince until their noses nearly touched. The newspaper reporter's camera clicked away.

"Bailey City belongs to me!" Bear Claw yelled into Viking Vince's face.

"Not as long as I'm champion," Viking Vince snarled and waved his arm around. The kids ducked before Vince could see them.

Bear Claw backed Vince into a corner. "You won't be champion for long," he said. "I plan on stripping you of that belt."

"This mangy bear cub can't win against me!" Vince yelled to the reporter. "Wait and see. *WrestleBaileyLive* will belong to the Vikings. This city and everything in it will be mine! MINE!"

One of Vince's Viking friends pulled him away from Bear Claw. "Save your fight for *WrestleBaileyLive*," Vince's friend said

as he pulled Vince toward the door. "It's time to go back to the gym."

"You'd better train hard this afternoon!" Bear Claw warned. "You'll need every ounce of strength to fight me for the championship!"

Vince strained to get away from his trainer but the other two Vikings rushed to pull him out of Burger Doodle. The newspaper reporter kept taking pictures until they were out of sight.

"Tomorrow is Friday," Liza whimpered. "You know what that means, don't you?"

Howie nodded. "We don't have much time," he said, "to stop a Viking invasion!"

8

Ready Eddie the Terrible

"Let's get out of here while we still can," Howie suggested. The kids slipped out the door while the rest of the wrestlers finished cramming Doodle Burgers in their mouths.

Howie pulled his friends into the shadow of a building once they were away from Burger Doodle. "We have to stop Vince from conquering Bailey City," he told his friends.

Melody shook her head so hard her pigtails bopped Eddie on the nose. "We can't stop the wrestling match. After all, your parents have been trying to stop it for days and they haven't had any luck."

"Besides," Eddie said, "why do you want to stop wrestling?"

"I'm not worried about wrestling,"

Howie said. "I'm scared of a real Viking who is planning to invade Bailey City with all his Viking friends."

"But we don't know that Vince is really a Viking," Liza pointed out.

"That's right," Melody said. "After all, wrestlers are known for getting attention by doing and saying silly things."

Howie held up his hand. "Didn't you hear what Vince said?" Howie asked. "He said Bear Claw was no match against the Vikings. That can only mean one thing. More Vikings are on their way and Vince is planning on leading a Viking invasion right here in Bailey City."

"I think real Vikings in Bailey City would be great," Eddie said. "I could join them and be Ready Eddie the Terrible. I'm going to start cramming whole hamburgers and piles of french fries into my mouth right away!"

Liza grabbed Eddie's arm. "You'd better not," she said. "That could be dangerous."

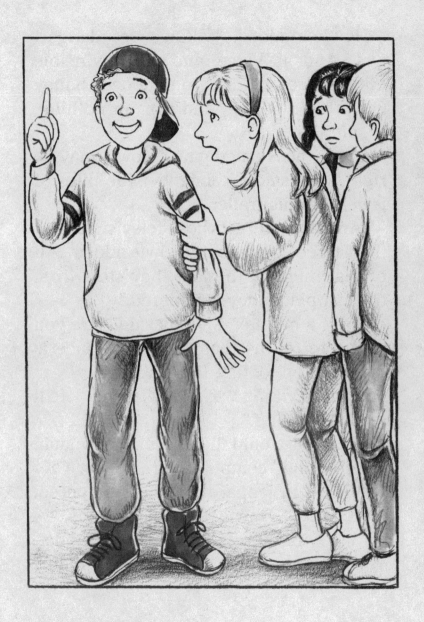

Howie nodded. "Vikings are danger-ous. And if Vince and his invincible Vikings are planning to take over Bailey City, then nothing, and I mean nothing, is safe."

Liza's face turned pale. "Howie may be right," she said. "Remember the piles of jewelry in his trailer."

"And don't forget those televisions and that stereo equipment," Howie added. "All of that must be the loot they stole from the last place they conquered."

"Wait a minute," Melody said. "Are you trying to tell us that you think Vince is planning on looting Bailey City?"

"It's the Viking way," Howie said. "He'll stop at nothing."

"But that would mean every television, watch, and computer in Bailey City would be in jeopardy," Liza whimpered.

"Exactly," Howie told his friends. "A Viking's mission is to loot and plunder. When Vince pulls out of town, Bailey

City will be emptied of everything that's valuable."

Eddie staggered back until he fell against the wall of a nearby building. "Not my television," he gasped. "Not my computer games."

Howie put his hand on Eddie's shoulder. "You heard him yourself. Viking Vince is planning to take over Bailey City until everything in it belongs to him."

"What can we do?" Eddie asked.

Howie reached above Eddie's head and snatched a sign about the wrestling match off the side of the building. He shook the paper in front of his friends. "We have to be at the first day of wrestling on Friday," he said, "even if it's the last thing we do!"

9

A to Z

"Our parents will never let us go to the match," Liza said.

"I can go anywhere, anytime," Eddie bragged.

"That's not true, and you know it," Howie pointed out. "If your grandmother caught you sneaking into *WrestleBaileyLive* without her permission, you would end up copying the encyclopedia from A to Z!"

Melody snatched the paper from Howie's hand. "Our parents may not want us to go to the match," Melody said slowly, "but did they ever say anything about going to practice?"

"What practice?" Liza asked.

Melody pointed down the street. The rest of the wrestlers were pouring out of

Burger Doodle Restaurant. They looked like a monster parade as they marched down the street toward the high school. "Remember what Bear Claw told Vince? He said he needed to train this afternoon. I bet that's where they're going right now."

"What good will sneaking into the practice do?" Liza asked.

"It's always good to know your enemy before you do battle," Howie said.

"Enemy?" Liza yelped. "This is getting way too serious. Maybe we should tell our parents."

"Our parents won't believe us until it's too late," Howie said. "That's why we have to keep an eye on things. At the first sign of a Viking invasion we'll warn everybody. It's up to us to save Bailey City."

Melody nodded. "Follow me," she told them. "But don't make a sound." The kids kept to the shadows, careful not to let any of the wrestlers or picketing parents see them. They waited until most of the wrestlers had either entered the high school gym or disappeared into their trailers. Then the kids sneaked in a door at the back of the gym and hid behind the bleachers. From their hiding place, they had a clear view of the wrestling ring.

Vince was there, along with some of the other wrestlers. CaveMonster and Apeman stood in the ring, but it didn't look like they were wrestling. The two wrestlers grasped arms and slowly circled the ring.

"Why are they moving so slowly?" Eddie asked. "It looks like they're dancing a ballet instead of wrestling."

"Wrestling is like dancing," Melody told him. "There are certain moves they practice."

Eddie watched as CaveMonster leaped across the ring and barely tapped Apeman on the shoulder. Apeman sank to the floor in slow motion.

"But that's like telling a fib," Eddie argued.

Howie slapped Eddie on the back. "You should know. After all, you're the master of telling stories."

"People who come to wrestling matches want to see action," Eddie blurted, "not dancing."

"Now you understand why honesty *is* the best policy," Liza said.

"I thought wrestlers were the power-houses of all athletes," Eddie said sadly. "But I guess you were right all along."

"Wrestlers *are* athletes," Howie pointed out. "It takes a lot of skill and strength to do what they do. Even if it isn't for real."

Melody nodded. "Just look at those muscles," she said as CaveMonster grabbed Apeman under his arms. He lifted Apeman clear off the floor. Before he could drop him, Apeman wrapped a long jungle vine around his head.

"I sure wouldn't want to tangle with any of them," Melody added.

Eddie backed away. "You're right," he said as his friends followed him outside

into the cold air. "I wouldn't want to tangle with a group of dancers, either."

"They're not dancers," Howie said. "Just because they practice certain moves, it doesn't mean they're not dangerous."

"I don't care if they're really wrestling or not," Liza said. "Mrs. Scott was right. Brainpower is better than fighting. I think wrestling is dangerous. Especially when the champion wrestler is a Viking planning to take over Bailey City."

"I agree with Liza," Melody said, pulling her friends to a stop. "We don't have to worry about wrestlers. We need to worry about Vikings!"

Howie nodded. "If Vince's Vikings invade *WrestleBaileyLive*, Bailey City will be taken by total surprise. We have to be there to warn people, no matter what!"

10

Heroes

Melody, Howie, Eddie, and Liza paused on the library steps. It was the next afternoon and they had gone to the library as soon as school let out, but they hadn't stayed long. The gargoyles on the roof glared down at the four kids as they zipped up their jackets. "I'm not so sure this is a good idea," Liza said. "What if our parents find out?"

"Did your mother ever tell you not to go?" Melody asked Liza.

"No," Liza said slowly, "but I know she wouldn't like it."

"By the time they find out," Eddie said, "we'll be heroes. Besides, we're not really telling a lie about being at the library."

"That's true," Howie said, patting his

stuffed backpack. "We really did get books for our report on ancient Greece and the Olympics."

"Who cares about reports about old people?" Eddie said. "I'm ready to see exciting wrestling action."

"Do you really think we should sneak into today's wrestling match?" Liza asked. "Maybe we should do our homework instead."

Howie slipped on his backpack. "The only way we'll be able to warn everybody of a Viking invasion is if we're at that wrestling match. Now, let's stop arguing about it and go!"

The four kids skipped down the library steps and hurried away. They didn't say a word until they were in front of the high school. Bright lights shone on a sign for *WrestleBaileyLive* and the parking lot was jam-packed. A steady stream of people were buying tickets and entering the school's gym. That didn't stop a handful of parents from picketing. They

carried signs and marched in circles near the entrance.

"How are we going to get in without our parents seeing us?" Liza asked.

"Don't worry," Eddie said. "Nobody is going to notice four kids in that long line."

Eddie was right. Not one parent noticed they were standing in line. Nobody said a word as they paid for their tickets. The kids walked into the gym without a single problem.

"That was the easy part," Liza said. "Now we have to battle Vikings."

Howie shook his head and pointed to a cluster of police officers standing near the entrance to the gym. "We're not going to fight anybody," Howie said. "We just need to be ready to point out the Vikings when they show up. We'll let the guards do the rest. Right, Eddie? Eddie?"

Howie looked around. Eddie was nowhere to be found.

Melody looked like she was ready to

be sick. "We'd better find Eddie before he gets into trouble," she said.

"How did he get away so fast?" Liza said. They were used to Eddie getting into mischief, but not this quickly.

"There he is!" Howie cried. Liza and Melody followed Howie to the gym. Eddie was already looking for a seat so he could watch the wrestlers face off.

"We need to stick together," Melody warned Eddie.

Liza nodded. "Friends always stay together, no matter what."

"Then stick with me," Eddie told them as he squeezed around two teenagers to find some empty seats. The kids had barely sat down before the crowd jumped up to cheer.

Apeman stood in the middle of the ring. He beat his chest and grunted at Bear Claw. Both wrestlers started circling each other.

"That's the wrestler who challenged Vince," Melody said. "He's one of the best wrestlers here. If anybody can win that belt, it's Bear Claw."

"That means we should cheer for him," Liza said.

But Eddie didn't hear her. He was standing on his chair acting like a gorilla. He scratched his belly. He patted his head. He jumped up and down and grunted.

Howie tried to pull Eddie off the chair. Eddie refused to budge. "We're not here to watch the wrestling," Howie reminded him. "We're here to look for Vikings."

Just then, Bear Claw grabbed Apeman and threw him against the ropes.

"Did you see that?" Liza asked. "That was totally fake."

"No, it wasn't," Eddie argued. "Those wrestlers are really fighting."

The blood drained from Liza's face. "Maybe we should just go home," she said.

"We can't give up now," Howie told Liza. "We have to save Bailey City."

Apeman let out a King Kong roar and rolled toward Bear Claw. The crowd cheered as Bear Claw jumped out of the way. Bear Claw grabbed Apeman and trapped him in a headlock.

"I don't care about Bailey City," Eddie yelled down from his chair. "Life without television would be like life without sunshine or water or air! We have to save my TV!"

Liza put her hands on her hips and looked up at Eddie. "Television isn't *that* important," she said. "Maybe you should watch less TV and do more homework."

Eddie gasped. He grabbed his throat. He sank down to his chair. "Homework instead of TV?" he moaned. "Are you nuts?"

Howie stepped between Eddie and Liza and shook his head. "Liza isn't crazy," he said, "but Vince is!"

11

Honest-to-Goodness Truth

The crowd grew silent when Vince entered the gym. His trainers and manager were right behind him. They all wore leather helmets and long flowing capes.

"Put him down!" Viking Vince yelled to Bear Claw as he pushed his way into the ring.

When Bear Claw dropped Apeman as if he were a sack of potatoes, the audience gasped. Apeman bounced up and down on the mat but Vince just stepped over him and stomped toward Bear Claw. Neither of them looked happy.

"Oh, no," Liza groaned. "Vince couldn't wait for his match tomorrow. We're caught in the middle of a Viking showdown!"

"Don't worry," Melody said. "I'm pretty sure this isn't for real."

"It looks real to me," Liza said.

Vince and Bear Claw circled each other. The crowd chanted, wanting to see them fight for the belt.

Melody shook her head. "Wait and see. The referees will break this up. That way everybody will be sure to come back tomorrow night to see them wrestle for the belt."

One referee shouted at the wrestlers. Then three referees jumped in the ring, pulling Bear Claw and Vince away from each other.

"You were right," Liza said with a sigh of relief. "This was all just an act to get people to come back tomorrow."

Eddie looked at the wrestlers in the ring. Bear Claw jumped up and stomped hard on the mat. The entire ring shook, but the referee held on tight to his arm. "If the whole thing is an act, then that means Vince isn't really a Viking," Eddie

said slowly, thinking hard as he said it. "That means he's not invincible, either. After all, I'm pretty sure Vikings don't wear wrestling belts."

"I'm not so sure," Howie said. "But we have to find out before tomorrow's match if we plan to save Bailey City."

"No problem," Eddie said. "I'll find out right now!" Before his friends could stop him, Eddie jumped out of his chair and darted across the floor. The crowd gasped when Eddie jumped into the wrestling ring with Invincible Vince and Bear Claw. Referees still held Bear Claw and Vince apart.

"We have to save him," Liza yelled.

Howie gulped. "Don't look at me. I can't even beat a first-grader at arm wrestling." He held up a puny arm as proof.

"Let's just leave and pretend we don't know Eddie," Melody suggested.

Liza grabbed Howie and Melody, pulling them toward the ring. "Come on,"

Liza said. "Friends who stick together are stronger."

"Stronger than vicious Vikings?" Howie asked, his voice squeaking just a little.

Liza looked each of her friends in the eyes before taking a deep breath. "We're about to find out."

Liza, Melody, and Howie ignored the yelling crowd as they crawled into the ring and looked over Eddie's shoulders.

Eddie put both hands on his hips and looked Vince right in the eye. "Are you a real Viking?" Eddie bravely asked Vince.

Vince threw back his head and laughed at Eddie. "I am as real as they come. I dare you to look at my muscles and accuse me of being anything less."

Eddie drew himself up to his full height, which only came to Vince's belly button. "Your muscles won't be any good when I warn the rest of Bailey City about you," Eddie said, poking Vince's belt with a finger.

Liza fell backward, ready to faint. "Oh, no," she gasped. "This is it."

Howie's lip started quivering. "Say good-bye to Eddie," he said.

"Maybe I should run and get help," Melody said with a trembling voice.

"Hurry!" Liza said. "Before it's too late."

Melody turned to get out of the ring, but she didn't get far. She ran right into a solid wall of muscle named Bear Claw.

"You have crossed me once too often," Vince roared at Bear Claw over the kids' heads. "We will settle this once and for all. I challenge you to a battle tomorrow night before the great citizens of Bailey City."

"Done," Bear Claw said, eyeing Vince's belt. "Winner takes all!"

Vince roared past the kids and jumped from the mat. He stormed out of the gym, leaving Liza trembling. But nobody noticed.

The crowd cheered. They yelled. They

hollered. Especially one lady sitting in the front row.

"Uh-oh," Eddie said, pointing to the cheering crowd.

Melody, Liza, and Howie looked where Eddie pointed. "What's your grandmother doing here?" Melody squealed.

"I'm doomed," Eddie moaned. "It won't matter if Vikings take over Bailey City. I'll never see another television again in my life!"

12

Brainpower

Melody, Liza, and Howie met Eddie extra early at the library the next day.

"Was it terrible?" Liza asked Eddie.

"Will you survive?" Howie asked.

"Is there any way we can help you?" Melody asked. "What did your grandmother say?"

Eddie shook his head. "My grandmother is one tough cookie," he said. "She told me she would have let me come to the match if only I'd asked. But I didn't ask. I lied. Now I have to copy one page from every volume in the encyclopedia before I'm allowed to watch television ever again."

"That won't matter," Howie said sadly. "Since we were caught, we can't go back to see the Main Event tonight. Viking

Vince and his invaders are bound to take over Bailey City anyway. Say good-bye to television forever."

"Don't be so sure," Liza said cheerfully.

"Why?" Howie said. "Do you know something we don't know?"

Liza giggled and pointed to a convoy of wrestling trailers turning the corner and driving past the library.

"Where are they going?" Eddie shouted. "Viking Vince hasn't wrestled yet!"

Liza shook her head and smiled even bigger. "Our wrestling worries are over. Viking Vince won't be wrestling Bear Claw — at least not in Bailey City."

"Why not?" Howie asked.

"Because I battled the Vikings all on my own," Liza said with a smug grin. "And I won!"

"No way," Eddie said. "You couldn't beat a kitten in a tug-of-war!"

"I may not be the best athlete in Bailey City," Liza agreed, "but I didn't need

muscles to save Bailey City from the Vikings. I used something even better. Brainpower!"

"What are you talking about?" Melody asked.

"It was easy," Liza said. "I suggested to my mom that Sheldon City would love to host a wrestling match. It's bigger and has more businesses that could sponsor the wrestlers. Mom thought it was a great idea and got on the phone. When Sheldon City High School offered the wrestlers a better deal, Vince and his pals jumped at the chance. In no time flat, they picked up and left."

Howie slapped Liza on her back. "You're right," he told her. "You saved Bailey City from a Viking invasion!"

"We don't know that for sure," Eddie complained. "We never proved Vince was a Viking. And now, thanks to Liza, we don't even get to watch Vince defend his belt!"

"Well," Howie said slowly, "if you

really aren't too afraid to find out, why don't you get your grandmother to take you to Sheldon City?"

Eddie kicked at the library step. His face turned as red as his hair. "I won't have time," he said a little too quickly. "I'll be too busy copying stuff from the encyclopedia."

"Maybe some things are better when you just pretend," Liza said with a giggle.

"Like wrestling," Melody added with a laugh, "and Vikings!"

Debbie Dadey and Marcia Thornton Jones have fun writing together. When they both worked at an elementary school in Lexington, Kentucky, Debbie was the school librarian and Marcia was a teacher. During their lunch break in the school cafeteria, they came up with the idea of the Bailey School Kids.

Recently Debbie and her family moved to Aurora, Illinois. Marcia and her husband still live in Kentucky, where she continues to teach. How do these authors still write together? They talk on the phone and use computers and fax machines!

Learn more about Debbie and Marcia on their Web site: www.BaileyKids.com